ONLINE A

THE ORCHARD BOOK OF
Funny Fairy Tales

For Cathy, with love – 35 fairytale years
L.A.

In memory of Elaine, with love
A.R.

Visit the Anholt website: www.anholt.co.uk

ORCHARD BOOKS
338 Euston Road, London NW1 3BH
Orchard Books Australia
Level 17/207 Kent Street, Sydney, NSW 2000

First published in 2013 by Orchard Books

A CIP catalogue record for this book
is available from the British Library.

ISBN 978 1 40830 764 9

1 3 5 7 9 10 8 6 4 2

Printed in China

Orchard Books is a division of Hachette Children's Books,
an Hachette UK company.
www.hachette.co.uk

THE ORCHARD BOOK OF
Funny Fairy Tales

Laurence Anholt
Arthur Robins

ORCHARD

CONTENTS

Cinderella
and the
Stinky Stepsisters

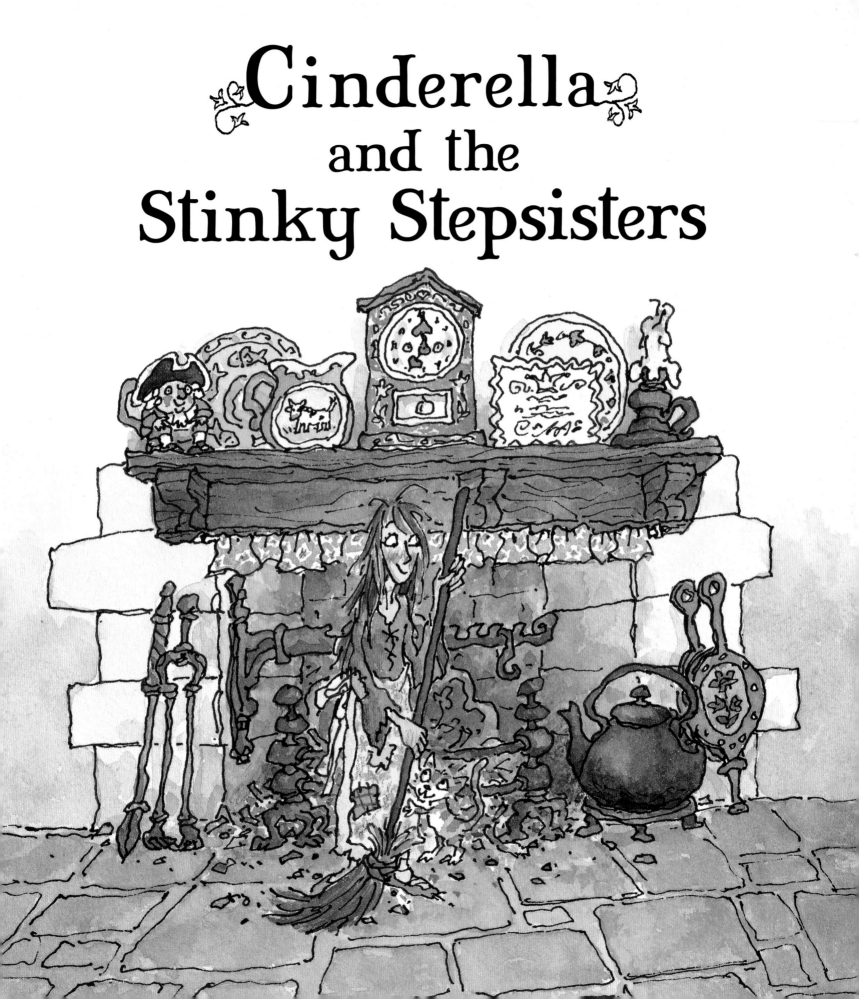

There were once three stinky stepsisters. Their names were Bumblegrump, Snoozethimble and Twitpin. One was short, one was tall and one was wide. They spent all day squabbling and pulling each other's hair.

"She did it!"

"No, she did it!"

"I wasn't even there!"

"She did it!"

"No, she did it!"

"It's just NOT FAIR!"

The three stinky stepsisters were very spoilt. Their poor father spent all his money buying them expensive dresses and everything their greedy hearts desired.

Now, their father had one other daughter who was very different indeed. She was the sweetest, kindest girl you could ever meet, but the three stinky stepsisters treated her very badly. While they slept in soft, warm beds, the poor girl had to curl up with the cats in the cinders by the fire. So, everyone called her Cinderella.

Day after day, Cinderella washed and cooked and ironed and cleaned, while the stinky stepsisters did nothing except squabble.

Early one morning, the postman arrived looking very excited. He was holding a large envelope.

"LOOK! LOOK!" he shouted.

"A letter from the palace!"

"My letter!"

"No, my letter!"

"You weren't even there!"

"My letter!"

"My letter!"

"It's just NOT FAIR!"

The stinky stepsisters were no good at reading, so they made Cinderella read the letter aloud.

Step right up for the Fairytale Ball –
the King and Queen invite you all.
Our charming son requires a bride
(she may be short or tall or wide).
So, give your hair a special rinse,
come and meet the handsome prince.
Send a text or give a ring.
With lots of love,
the Queen and King

The stinky stepsisters were terribly excited.

"The prince will dance with me," sighed Bumblegrump.

"The prince will fall in love with me," sighed Snoozethimble.

"The prince will marry me," sighed Twitpin.

"Whatever will we wear?" sighed Cinderella.

"WHAT?" shouted the stinky stepsisters. "Cinderella at the royal palace? With her tattered clothes and her tangly hair? You might as well invite the mice from the kitchen floor . . . or that kitten sleeping by the fire! Of course *you* won't go to the ball."

The stinky stepsisters bullied their father into buying them expensive dresses, and when the evening of the ball arrived, Cinderella helped her sisters get ready and told them how lovely they looked.

Bumblegrump, Snoozethimble and Twitpin stepped into their carriage, squabbling all the time.

"Don't forget to tidy the house while we are gone," they shouted to Cinderella. Then their father drove the stinky stepsisters out of the drive and down the road to the palace.

Poor Cinderella was left all alone. The house was very quiet. She set about tidying all the mess her sisters had left and, at last, she curled up exhausted by the fire. She dreamt she was dancing with the prince. A small tear rolled down her cheek, into the warm cinders.

Suddenly, there was a flash of light. The fire burned so bright that Cinderella could hardly see. Then she heard a funny voice.

"Don't cry, Cinderella."

"Who's there?" cried Cinderella, rubbing her eyes.

A funny lady stood in the middle of the kitchen floor. She looked kind, but all her clothes were in a muddle.

"I am your hairy frogmother," she said. "I mean your fairy godmother. I'm sorry; I get so muddled. Why are you crying, Cinderella?"

"I am crying because everyone has gone to the Fairytale Ball," said Cinderella. "I dreamt of dancing with the prince."

"Well, Cinderbrella, tonight you shall prance with the dunce . . . I mean dance with the prince."

"Oh," sighed Cinderella, "but how would I get to the ball?"

"Go to the garden and pump me a pipkin . . . I mean pick me a pumpkin," said the fairy godmother.

Cinderella did what she was told and found her fairy godmother a huge pumpkin. The old lady waved her wand and made some mixed-up magic –

"Pimpkin pumpkin on a dish,
Meddle muddle, make a wish."

Cinderella couldn't believe her eyes – in a flash, the pumpkin changed into a beautiful carriage.

"But who will pull the carriage?" asked Cinderella.

"Just bring me six metal lice . . . I mean six little mice,"
said the fairy godmother.

Cinderella caught six little mice and
her fairy godmother made more mixed-up magic –

"Meddle muddle magic mice,
Six white horses would be nice."

In a flash, the six little mice changed into magnificent
horses, ready to pull the carriage.

"But who will drive the carriage?" asked Cinderella.

"Just bring me that sleepy kipper by the fire," replied her fairy godmother.

"I think you mean the sleepy kitten," laughed Cinderella.

"Meddle muddle magic cat,
Become a coachman with a hat."

Cinderella stared in amazement as her kitten changed into a handsome coachman, waiting to drive her away.

Then Cinderella looked down at her tattered clothes and her worn-out shoes.

"Oh, Fairy Godmother! What shall I wear to the ball?" she sighed.

"A gorgeous gall bown, of course," said her fairy godmother –

"With skin as soft as buttermilk,
Your tattered rags will turn to silk."

Cinderella walked to the mirror. At first, she did not recognise the beautiful girl she saw. She was dressed from head to foot in the finest silken clothes, with glistening jewels and shining hair. And on her feet were the most perfect slippers made of sparkling glass.

"Oh, thank you!" gasped Cinderella, kissing her fairy godmother and climbing into the coach.

"But there is one thing you must not forget," called her muddily fairy godmother. "Before the tock strikes twelve, you must curry to your heart . . . I mean hurry to your cart. That is when the magic will end."

Cinderella promised she would remember. Then the coachman, who looked a little like her kitten, raised his hat, and the pumpkin carriage flew into the night.

It seemed like seconds before they pulled up outside the palace, where fireworks lit up the sky. Cinderella felt very nervous. She could hear music and laughter inside. She climbed slowly up the steps and into the ballroom. As she stepped inside, five hundred people stood and stared. The music stopped. The dancers froze. Every eye was fixed on the beautiful girl with the glass slippers.

Cinderella saw Bumblegrump, Snoozethimble and Twitpin squabbling over who would dance with the prince. Of course, they did not recognise Cinderella.

Then Cinderella saw Prince Charming. He was the most handsome man she had ever seen . . . and he was staring at her!

"Whoever is that lovely girl?" he sighed. "Take me away from these awful sisters."

When Cinderella danced with the prince, the glass slippers
made her feet feel as light as air.
The hours slipped away and
it was the most wonderful
evening of her life.
As she danced,
her muddily old fairy
godmother seemed
a million miles away.

Cinderella knew there was
something she had promised, but she
couldn't think what it was. But,
as the clock began to strike
midnight, she remembered!

Cinderella hurried across
the ballroom. She ran so fast
that one slipper fell from her
foot. As the clock struck twelve,
she ran into the dark night.

A pumpkin sat where her carriage had been. Six little mice scampered at her feet. Her beautiful dress had gone and Cinderella stood dressed in rags once more. She felt something brush against her legs, and there was her little kitten. She picked him up and carried him home through the cold night.

When the stinky stepsisters returned, Cinderella was curled up with the kitten by the fire. They shook her awake to put away their clothes and told her about the night at the ball.

"The prince was just about to dance with me," groaned Bumblegrump, "when in walked the most beautiful girl you have ever seen – a princess for sure."

"He forgot all about us," complained Snoozethimble. "They danced together all night and he was heartbroken when she ran away."

"All she left was one glass slipper," moaned Twitpin, "but the prince will not rest until he has found her."

Cinderella smiled gently. Even if she never saw the prince again, she would always remember the Fairytale Ball.

Early next day, there was a loud knock at the door. Outside stood a group of finely dressed servants, and at the front was Prince Charming himself, holding a glass slipper –

"Whoever fits her foot inside,
That lovely girl shall be my bride."

"Oh, that'll be me, Your Highness," said Bumblegrump, coming down the stairs in her pyjamas.

"No, Your Highness, I was the beautiful one," said Snoozethimble.

"Here I am, my prince," called Twitpin. "I'll just pack a bag."

"Oh," said the prince. "Of course you are all lovely, but I am looking for the princess who dropped this glass slipper."

"I dropped it!"

"No, I dropped it!"

"She wasn't even there!"

"I dropped it!"

"No, I dropped it!"

"It's just NOT FAIR!"

First Bumblegrump tried the slipper, but her foot was too short.

Then Snoozethimble tried, but her foot was too long.

Then Twitpin tried, but her foot was too wide.

"Thank you, ladies," said the prince. "I am sorry to have disturbed you."

He turned to leave, but just at that moment, one of his men noticed a girl in tattered clothes sitting quietly by the fire with a kitten in her lap.

"Oh, that's just Cinderella," laughed the sisters. "She sleeps by the fire. She's no princess!"

Nonetheless, the prince held out the glass slipper and Cinderella stepped forward.

With no effort at all, she slid her foot inside the glass slipper.

It fitted perfectly!

"But she wasn't even at the ball!" shrieked the stinky stepsisters.

The prince held out his hands and smiled at Cinderella –

**"Cinderella, please decide,
If you would like to be my bride."**

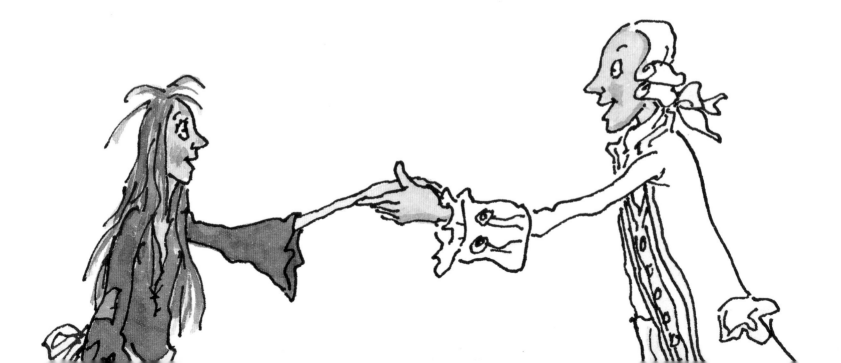

Cinderella was so happy that a tear of joy fell from her eye into the cinders by the fire. Suddenly there was a flash of light and there stood her fairy godmother. She waved her wand and Cinderella's rags changed into a silk wedding dress.

The stinky stepsisters stared in amazement. Then they began to boast about how kind they had been to Cinderella.

Cinderella went to live in the fairytale palace. She brought her father and her little kitten and, being as kind as she was beautiful, she invited Bumblegrump, Snoozethimble and Twitpin to live there too.

And the most important guest at the wedding was
Cinderella's muddily fairy godmother –

"That's the end now, meddle muddle,
So give that prince a lovely cuddle."

Silly
Jack
and the
Beanstalk

There was once a silly boy named Jack.

He was always giggling.

"Hee-hee-hee-hello!"

Jack wore a hat with JACK on the front so he would never forget his name. His best friend was a cow named Milky White. They played together all day long and got really dirty. In the evening, they played in the bath, put on their pyjamas and hopped into their bunk beds.

Jack and his mum were very poor. All they had to eat was what Milky gave them, and Jack's mum hated milk.

"All we eat is milk and yoghurt."

"And chee-hee-heese, Mum!"

Jack didn't mind. He loved milk. He could drink it all day long. But his mum dreamt about all the lovely food she would buy if they were rich ... **hot chocolate roly-poly with chocolate custard and chocolate buttons on top** ...

Then, one day, something terrible happened – Milky White ran out of milk!

"Well, that's that, Jack. No more milk or yoghurt."

"Or chee-hee-heese, Mum!"

Jack and his mum had nothing at all to eat.

"If only you weren't so silly, Jack," said his mum, "you would think of a way to make some money."

In the middle of the night, something strange happened – Jack had an idea. He had never had an idea before, so it felt very funny. He sat up in his bunk bed and banged his head on Milky White's bottom. Then Milky White sat up and banged her head on the ceiling.

"Listen, Milky," said Jack. "I will take you to the market and sell you. Then Mum can buy lots of lovely things to eat."

Poor Milky White didn't want to be sold. "Moo-hoo-hoo!" she said. But Jack promised that as soon as he was rich, he would buy Milky White back again.

Jack was so excited he couldn't sleep. In the morning, he told his mum about his idea.

"Oh, Jack!" she said. "Perhaps you are growing up at last."

She took a piece of string and tied one end to Jack's belt. Then she tied the other end around Milky White's neck so they wouldn't lose each other.

"Now, Jack, you must remember three things," she said. "First, you must not tell anyone that Milky White cannot make milk. Otherwise no one will want her at all."

"You can trust me-hee-hee!" giggled Jack.

"Second, you must bring back lots of delicious things for us to eat."

"We'll have a lovely tea-hee-hee!" giggled Jack.

"And most important, Jack," said his mum, "you must not be silly."

"I agree-hee-hee!" giggled Jack.

So, Jack and Milky White set off along the path that led through the hills and into the town.

They had only been walking for five minutes when they met a small round wizard sitting beside the road.

"Hello, Jack," said the small round wizard. Jack wondered how the wizard knew his name.

"Hee-hee-hello, small round wizard," he giggled.

"Where are you off to so early in the morning?" asked the small round wizard.

"Hee-hee!" giggled Jack. "I am taking Milky White to the market. I must not tell anyone that she cannot make milk, otherwise no one will want her at all."

"Quite right," said the small round wizard. "Mind you, she's a fine-looking cow. I will buy her from you, milk or no milk."

"Hee-hee!" giggled Jack. "But I promised my mum I would bring back lots of delicious things to eat."

"This must be your lucky day!" said the small round wizard. "I have five delicious things, right here in my pocket. Look! Five yummy beans! I will swap them for your cow."

"Hee-hee!" giggled Jack. "I must be the luckiest boy alive."

"I can see you are a very clever boy," said the small round wizard. "So I'll tell you something else – these are not ordinary beans.

They are MAGIC BEANS!"

Jack was delighted. He put the beans carefully in his hat and kissed Milky White. "Goodbye, old bean!" Then he skipped all the way home.

"That was quick," said Jack's mum as Jack ran into the kitchen.

Jack couldn't wait to spill the beans and tell his mum how clever he had been.

"What?" she said. "You silly boy! You sold our cow for five beans?"

"It's all right, Mum," giggled Jack. "They are magic be-hee-heans!"

"I'll give you magic beans," said Jack's mum. She grabbed Jack's hat and tossed the beans as far as she could into the garden.

That night, poor Jack went to bed without even a glass of milk. Even worse, he didn't have Milky White to keep him company.

Early the next morning, a funny thing happened. Something long and green wiggled through the window and tickled Jack on his nose.

"Hee-hee-hee!" he giggled.

Jack jumped up, ran to the window and peeped outside. He couldn't believe his eyes! The five beans had grown into five beanstalks, all wrapped around each other. It was . . .

THE BIGGEST BEANSTALK IN THE WORLD!

Jack got dressed and ran outside. The beanstalk was still
growing – higher and higher it climbed, twisting around,
like a great green ladder reaching far into the clouds.
From every branch hung soft green leaves, and
under each leaf hung beans as big as boats.

There was only one thing to do.
Jack put on his hat and began to
climb – up, and up, and up
the magic beanstalk.
And as he climbed,
he sang a song –

"Hee-hee-hee!
Look at me!
Climbin' up the beanstalk.
I didn't mean,
To plant a bean,
Now I'm climbin' up the beanstalk."

Way down below, Jack could see his tumbledown cottage and his mum, as small as a raisin, waving up at him. All day, Jack climbed higher. The birds swooped around his head and small clouds tickled his ears.

At last, just when he thought he could climb no higher, Jack saw the tip of the beanstalk waggling through a hole in the clouds. He crawled into the sky and found himself in Cloudland.

As far as he could see, a wonderful colourful world stretched before him. There were marshmallow hills scattered with candyfloss sheep under a sparkling starlit sky. He saw cotton wool trees and milkshake streams. A winding road led through the countryside towards an ice cream mountain, and on top of the ice cream mountain stood the biggest castle Jack had ever seen.

Jack may have been a silly boy, but he was very brave.

He crept slowly forward, along the winding road.

Then he began to climb –

    up,

       and up,

          and up the mountain.

And as he went, he sang a song –

"Hee-hee-hee!

Look at me!

I'm such a naughty rascal.

It's like a dream,

Made of ice cream,

Now I'm climbin' to the castle."

At the top of the mountain was a door as big as a football field.

Jack shook in his shoes. An enormous sign was hanging on the door –

FUM! FO! FI! FEE!
COME INSIDE
AND HAVE
SOME TEA!

Slowly, Jack crept inside the enormous castle. He wandered from room to room until he came to a colossal kitchen. Sitting in an armchair as big as a house was a huge giant.

"Hee-hee-HELP!" shouted Jack. But the giant was smiling.

"FUM! FO! FEE! FI! I'm the gentle giant, hi!"

The gentle giant poured a huge cup of tea for himself and a small cup of tea for Jack.

"FUM! FO! FEE! FI! Come on, Jack, don't be shy."

"I wonder how he knows my name," thought Jack. He climbed up to the chair and had tea with the gentle giant.

The giant was very polite.

"FEE! FO! FUM! FI! Would you like some apple pie?"

Jack told the gentle giant all about his life in the tumbledown cottage and about his best friend, Milky White, and the small round wizard and the huge beanstalk. The giant thought it was a very funny story. Then Jack thought about his mum, all by herself in the tumbledown cottage. He got up and shook hands with the gentle giant.

"See-hee-hee you later, Mr Giant!" he giggled.

The gentle giant stretched up to a high shelf and lifted down a cage.

"FEE! FI! FO! FUM! Here's a present for your mum."

He reached inside and pulled out a fat hen.

"Cluck, clack! Hello, Jack!" said the hen.

"How does she know my name?" wondered Jack.

Then the gentle giant gave Jack a big hug.

"FUM! FO! FEE! FI! Now it's time to say goodbye."

Jack walked back to the beanstalk. He climbed down,

and down,

and down,

with the fat hen in his arms.

And on the way, he sang a song –

"Hee-hee-hee!
Look at me!
Climbin' down the beanstalk.
My name's Jack,
I'm going back,
Climbin' down the beanstalk."

At last he reached the tumbledown cottage. His mum was very pleased to see him.

"Oh, Jack!" she cried. "Where have you bean?"

Jack told her all about the gentle giant and the castle in the sky.

"Hee-hee! Look, I've brought you a present," giggled Jack, and he gave her the fat hen.

"That's egg-sactly what I need!" said Jack's mum. "We'll have boiled eggs for tea."

Just at that moment, the hen laid an egg that was very hard indeed.

"Perhaps it's ha-ha-hard boiled!" giggled Jack.

"No!" said Jack's mum. "This egg is not hard boiled. This egg is made of GOLD!"

And it was true! Every egg the magic hen laid was made of solid gold.

So, Jack and his mum took a bag of golden eggs and set off to sell them at the market. Then Jack's mum bought loads of lovely things to eat ... strawberry mousse delight with sprinkly sugared almonds; hot chocolate roly~poly; wriggle~giggle~gooey cake.

Jack saw someone he knew. It was the small round wizard with his best friend, Milky White. Jack gave the small round wizard five golden eggs in return for Milky White.

Milky White was very pleased to see Jack, and Jack was very pleased to see Milky White.

They all lived happily ever after. Jack and Milky White and the fat hen played silly games all day long. And, every Sunday, the gentle giant came down from Cloudland and they all sat

together by the tumbledown cottage and told funny stories
and giggled and giggled and giggled.

"Hee-hee-hee! Have some more tea-hee-hee!"

The Big Tough "Billy Goats Gruff"

There were once three billy goats. Their names were Billy the Kid, Middle-Sized Mike and Big Tough Billy Goat Gruff.

Every night, Big Tough Billy Goat Gruff put his kids to bed, and every night, the billy goat boys hopped about and said, "Dad, Dad! Tell us a story!"

So, their dad began. "Well," said Big Tough Billy Goat Gruff, "when I was a kid, we went for a holiday in the mountains."

"What was it like, Dad?" asked Billy the Kid.

"Well," said Big Tough Billy Goat Gruff, "the air was sweet and the grass was green."

"What did you do, Dad?" asked Middle-Sized Mike.

"We chewed buttercups from morning till night until our billy goat bellies were full. And that's the end of the story."

But the billy goat boys hopped about and said, "Dad, Dad! Don't be a tease. Tell us about the troll!"

"Well," said Big Tough Billy Goat Gruff, "on our holiday, everyone was happy. Everyone except a grumpy troll."

"What was he like, Dad?" asked Billy the Kid.

"His face was green and his hair was blue and his nose was as long as a cucumber."

Then the billy goat boys laughed and laughed.

"Where did he live, Dad?" asked Middle-Sized Mike.

"Well," said Big Tough Billy Goat Gruff, "he lived under a rickety bridge, beside a gurgling stream."

"What did he do, Dad?" asked Billy the Kid.

"Do? He didn't do anything. He lay under the bridge and he snored and snored and snored."

Then the billy goat boys laughed and laughed and made the noise of snoring trolls.

"BUT!" said Big Tough Billy Goat Gruff. "If anyone stepped onto the rickety bridge – trip, trap, trip – UP POPPED THE TROLL!"

"What did he say, Dad?" asked the billy goat boys.

"WHO'S THAT TRIP TRAPPING OVER MY BRIDGE?" roared Big Tough Billy Goat Gruff.

Then Big Tough Billy Goat Gruff laughed and laughed, and Middle-Sized Mike laughed and laughed, and Billy the Kid laughed most of all.

Then Big Tough Billy Goat Gruff kissed the billy goat boys goodnight and they dreamt of the mountains, where the air is sweet and the grass is green.

One day, Big Tough Billy Goat Gruff said, "Guess what, boys? I've got a big surprise for you."

"What is it, Dad?" asked the billy goat boys.

"We're going on holiday!" said Big Tough Billy Goat Gruff. "We are off to the mountains where the air is sweet."

So, Billy the Kid packed a tiny bag and Middle-Sized Mike packed a middle-sized bag and Big Tough Billy Goat Gruff packed a huge big billy goat bag.

Then the billy goats locked up their house and climbed onto a train, which puffed and puffed out of the town and into the mountains. Billy the Kid and Middle-Sized Mike were so excited they hopped from seat to seat and would not sit still.

When the train stopped, Big Tough Billy Goat Gruff said, "Give me your bags, boys. Now you can run wherever you like!"

Billy the Kid jumped down and hopped along the path. Middle-Sized Mike shouted, "Wait for me!" but Billy the Kid was gone.

Billy the Kid ran fast. He ran around a corner. He saw a lovely buttercup field across a gurgling stream. Over the gurgling stream was a rickety bridge. Billy the Kid hopped onto the rickety bridge – trip, trap, trip . . .

Up popped the troll. His face was green, his hair was blue and his nose was as long as a cucumber.

"WHO'S THAT TRIP TRAPPING OVER MY BRIDGE?" he roared.

Billy the Kid just laughed. "I am Billy the Kid, and I've come to have a holiday."

Then the grumpy troll said –

"My nose is long, my hair is blue.
My favourite dinner looks like YOU!"

Billy the Kid was clever. "I will trick this grumpy troll," he thought.

"Oh, please don't eat me, Mr Troll," he said. "I am just a baby billy goat. I wouldn't even be a tiny snack for a great big troll like you. Wait a moment and my brother, Middle-Sized Mike, will come along. He is much tastier."

The grumpy troll thought for a moment, stroking his cucumber nose.

"You *are* very tiny," he agreed. "Hop off, quick, before I change my mind."

And he went back under the bridge and snored and snored.

Billy the Kid hopped into the buttercup field and he laughed and laughed.

Along came Middle-Sized Mike. He saw the lovely buttercup field across the gurgling stream. Middle-Sized Mike hopped onto the rickety bridge – trip, trap, trip . . .

Up popped the troll.

"WHO'S THAT TRIP TRAPPING OVER MY BRIDGE?" he roared.

Middle-Sized Mike just laughed. "I am Middle-Sized Mike, and I've come to have a holiday."

And the grumpy troll said –

**"My hair is blue, my face is green.
You're the tastiest dinner I've ever seen."**

"I will play a trick on this grumpy troll," thought Middle-Sized Mike.

"Oh, please don't eat me, Mr Troll," he said politely. "I am just a middle-sized billy goat. I am not a proper dinner for a great big troll like you. Just wait a moment and my dad, Big Tough Billy Goat Gruff, will be along. He is far tastier."

The grumpy troll thought for a moment, stroking his cucumber nose. "You are also not big enough," he agreed. "Hop off, quick, before I change my mind."

So, Middle-Sized Mike scampered into the buttercup field where Billy the Kid was waiting, and they laughed and laughed.

Along came Big Tough Billy Goat Gruff, carrying all the bags and the coats. He was singing a big tough billy goat song. He saw the lovely buttercup field across the gurgling stream, and he stepped onto the rickety bridge – TRIP, TRAP, TRIP! Big Tough Billy Goat Gruff was so big that the whole bridge began to shake.

Up popped the grumpy troll. "WHO'S THAT TRIP TRAPPING OVER MY BRIDGE?" he roared.

"It is ME!" said Big Tough Billy Goat Gruff. "I've come to have a holiday."

Then the troll stepped forward – THUMP! BUMP! GRUMP!

And Big Tough Billy Goat Gruff stepped forward – TRIP, TRAP, TRIP!

And the grumpy troll said –

**"The bridge is small and we are wide.
One of us must step aside."**

The grumpy troll pushed and shoved. But Big Tough Billy Goat Gruff only laughed. He put down his horns and he pushed and shoved until ...

SPLASH!

The grumpy troll fell
into the water!

**"I want my mum, I've had enough.
I'm not as tough as Billy Goat Gruff."**

Then Big Tough Billy Goat Gruff walked calmly and slowly over the rickety bridge and into the buttercup field, where the billy goat boys were waiting.

"Hooray!" shouted Middle-Sized Mike. "You're our hero, Dad!"

"Yes," said Billy the Kid, "you're the biggest, toughest, gruffest billy goat in the whole wide world."

Then they chewed buttercups from morning till night until their billy goat bellies were full.

And that's the end of the story.

Goldilocks
and the
Hairy Bears

There was once a little girl named Goldilocks. Goldilocks had beautiful golden hair, which tumbled down her back to her bottom.

One morning, Goldilocks went for a walk in the great green forest. She was singing a lovely song –

"With my golden hair and my frilly socks,
I am little Goldilocks."

She went further and further along the winding path –

"Pick some flowers, pat a fox,
I am little Goldilocks."

Deeper and deeper she went into the great green forest,
until she came to a sparkling river –

"Across the river, hopping rocks,
I am little Goldilocks."

But as she reached the other side, Goldilocks slipped and fell into the river with a splash!

"Oh!" she said. "I am cold and wet and . . . hungry!"

Just then, Goldilocks felt a little twitch in her nose. Something smelt delicious. "Mmm, porridge!"

Goldilocks followed her nose along the winding path until she found a pretty garden with a little green gate. She saw a wobbly house with a chimney and a bright blue door. The delicious smell was coming from inside.

Goldilocks stretched up to knock on the door –

"I'll give this knocker three good knocks.

I am little Goldilocks."

Goldilocks waited, but nobody answered the door.

"The people who live here must be out," she said. "I'll go inside and wait. No one will mind."

Goldilocks tiptoed into the wobbly house. She saw a sunny yellow kitchen with a big table and a bright fire.

"I'll stand by the fire and dry my dress," said Goldilocks. "No one will mind."

On the table were three steaming bowls of porridge.

"Mmm!" said Goldilocks. "My favourite! I'll just try a teeny-weeny bit. No one will mind."

First, Goldilocks tried the
GREAT BIG bowl.

"Oooh!" she said. "Far too hot!"

Then, she tried the
middle-sized bowl.

"Urgh!" said Goldilocks.

"Not sweet enough!"

Then, she tried the teeny-weeny bowl.

"Yum!" said Goldilocks. "This one is
exactly right. And even better with a big
blob of honey."

Then, she gobbled up every bit
and licked the last drip of honey from
the spoon.

"Yummy honey!" she said.

Then Goldilocks started to feel very tired.

"I wouldn't mind a little rest by the fire," she said.

"No one will mind."

Next to the fire were three chairs.

First, she tried the GREAT BIG chair. But it was so bouncy that she flew right off . . .

BOING!

Then, she tried the middle-sized chair.

But that was so soft and squashy, she tumbled right inside . . .

FLUMF!

Then, she tried the teeny-weeny chair. But it broke into
a hundred teeny-weeny pieces...

CRASH!

"That chair gave me a scare," said Goldilocks.

Then Goldilocks saw a staircase. There were three

clocks on the wall.

"I'll just tiptoe upstairs," she said. "No one will mind."

"Up the staircase, past the clocks,

Sleepy little Goldilocks."

At the top of the stairs was a tidy bathroom with three towels and three toothbrushes in three mugs. Next to the tidy bathroom was a cosy bedroom. In the cosy bedroom were three pairs of slippers and three dressing gowns and three neat beds.

Goldilocks yawned. "I'll just climb in and have a little nap. No one will mind."

There was a GREAT BIG bed, but that was far too bouncy. Goldilocks flew right off like a beach ball ...

BOING!

There was a middle-sized bed, but that was too soft and squashy. Goldilocks tumbled right inside ...

FLUMF!

Then, Goldilocks tried the teeny-weeny bed with the teeny-weeny pillow. And that was warm and snug. So, Goldilocks pulled up the covers and fell fast asleep, dreaming of warm porridge and honey.

While she was asleep, three bears on bicycles came pedalling through the trees. They had gone for a ride in the wood while their porridge was getting cool.

"WE WENT CYCLING IN THE WOOD."

"We left our breakfast as long as we could."

"Yum, that porridge smells so good!"

There was a GREAT BIG daddy bear on his GREAT BIG daddy bike. There was a middle-sized mummy bear on her middle-sized mummy bike and at the front was a teeny-weeny baby bear on a teeny-weeny baby bike with a bell. Ting-ting!

The three bears left their bikes by the gate and went inside the wobbly house.

"GR-RR-RR," grumbled Daddy Bear. "SOMEONE'S BEEN EATING MY PORRIDGE!"

"Ooh!" said Mummy Bear. "Someone's been eating my porridge too!"

"Boo-hoo!" cried Baby Bear.

"Someone's been eating *my* porridge . . . and they've eaten it all up!"

Then the three bears looked at their chairs.

"GR-RR-RR," grumbled Daddy Bear. "SOMEONE'S BEEN SITTING ON MY CHAIR!"

"Ooh!" said Mummy Bear. "Someone's been sitting on my chair too!"

"Boo-hoo!" cried Baby Bear. "Someone's been sitting on *my* chair . . . and they've broken it into teeny-weeny pieces!"

The three bears crept up the creaky stairs.

CREAK!
Creak!

Cre-ea-k!

Past the clocks and past the tidy bathroom they went. They crept into the cosy bedroom.

"GR-RR-RR!" growled Daddy Bear. "SOMEONE'S BEEN SLEEPING IN MY BED!"

"Ooh!" said Mummy Bear. "Someone's been sleeping in my bed too!"

"Boo-hoo!" cried Baby Bear. "Someone's been sleeping in *my* bed ... and THEY'RE STILL THERE!"

Goldilocks woke up. She sat up in bed. She rubbed her eyes –

"Oh my golly! What a scare!
I can see three hairy bears!"

But the bears were not cross. They were laughing.

"IT'S ONLY A LITTLE GIRL!" laughed Daddy Bear.

"She won't hurt anyone!" said Mummy Bear.

"Please can she stay and play?" squeaked Baby Bear.

"Yes," said Mummy Bear, "but first we must eat our porridge."

So, Mummy Bear gave Baby Bear a new bowl of porridge. Goldilocks was feeling hungry again, so she had another big bowl too. And they all ate every last bit.

"Mmm, yummy honey, Mummy!"

Then Goldilocks played with Baby Bear. They played
Musical Bears and had races up and down the garden.

"Ready, teddy, GO!"

At last, it was time for Goldilocks to go home.

"It's been nice meeting you," she said. "Thank you for
the porridge. Sorry about the chair."

Mummy Bear gave Goldilocks a big pot of porridge.

Daddy Bear gave Goldilocks a big bear hug and a jar
of honey.

And Baby Bear said Goldilocks could borrow his bike.

So, Goldilocks pedalled home through the great green

forest and through the sparkling river, singing as she went –

"I met three bears, I got three shocks,

I am little Goldilocks."

Along the winding path she cycled, all the way home.

And can you guess what she had for tea?

Šleeping Beauty
and the Funny Fairies

There was once a jolly king and a thin queen who were very happy and enormously rich. They had everything money could buy – a huge palace, a fast car, a hot-air balloon and loads of servants. But there was one thing they really wanted – a little fat baby!

One day, it was so hot that the jolly king took off his coat and put a block of ice in his crown, and the thin queen went swimming in the palace pool.

She left all her clothes on the side and hopped into the water.
Splash! Then the thin queen heard a funny voice –

**"I'm the froggy in the pool.
I am green and I am cool."**

"Oooh!" said the thin queen. "Who's in my pool?"

**"I'm the froggy in the water.
Within a year you'll have a daughter."**

The queen was so excited
that she jumped out of the cool
pool, pulled on all her clothes
without even getting dry and
ran to tell the king.

And guess what? The croaky
green frog was exactly right!
Before one year was over, the jolly king and the thin queen had a
bouncing baby girl. She was the fattest, jolliest, most beautiful baby
they had ever seen.

The jolly king and the thin
queen were so happy that they
decided to have a big party.
They invited every single
king, queen, prince and
princess for miles around.
They even invited the
croaky frog.

To make the party really special, the thin queen hired a tiny singing group called The Seven Good Fairies. The good fairies were terrific singers. They were terribly excited to be singing at the royal palace – they giggled and fluttered about all over the place.

The Seven Good Fairies sang a lovely song called 'Baby, Baby'. Each fairy made a magical wish for the fat little baby –

"Baby, baby, sweet and kind,
My wish for you is a clever mind."

"Baby, baby, boy, oh boy!
My wish for you is a life of joy."

"Baby, baby, here's my choice,
My wish for you is a lovely voice."

"Baby, baby, wrapped in lace,
My wish for you is a pretty face."

"Baby, baby, ribbons and bows,
I wish for you some groovy clothes."

"Baby, baby, before you're old,
My wish for you is a pile of gold."

"Baby, baby, until the end,
Each little fairy will be your friend."

The jolly king and the thin queen were delighted.
But, suddenly, the palace doors burst open and in came ...
the bad fairy.

You see, the singing group was really called The Seven Good
Fairies and One Bad Fairy, but the bad fairy had a cold that
day and she hadn't been invited in case she gave her nasty sore
throat to the princess. When the bad fairy saw all the presents
and lovely food, she was very cross indeed.

The bad fairy made her own wish for the new baby . . . and it was not a nice wish at all –

"Baby, baby, you'll cry and squeal,
When you prick your finger on a spinning wheel."

The thin queen was terribly upset, and even the king didn't look so jolly. But the bad fairy had not finished yet –

"Baby, baby, save your tears.
You will sleep for a hundred years."

Then the bad fairy laughed a croaky laugh, picked up
a whole plate of chocolate crispies
and fluttered out of the palace.

"What a meanie!"

"She's grumpy because she's poorly."

"We'll look after the princess."

"She's our friend."

"What can we do to help?"

"I know, why doesn't the king get
rid of ALL the spinning wheels?"

"Good idea, then the princess can't prick her finger at all!"

So, the jolly king ordered every spinning wheel in the land to be thrown onto a huge bonfire . . . except one, which he hid away in a secret tower, because, after all, the kingdom needed thread.

The little fat baby grew into a tall and beautiful princess. She had all the lovely things the fairies had wished for her – she was kind and happy and healthy, and everyone loved her.

One day, the jolly king and the thin queen went away to a pop festival. The Seven Good Fairies came to keep the princess company, and they all played hide-and-seek. When it was her turn to hide, the princess found a part of the palace with an interesting staircase that she had never seen before.

"They'll never find me up there," she giggled.

The princess crept up the stairs, all the way to the top. She saw a little door, and heard a funny noise coming from inside. *Squeak, squeak, squeak!*

The princess pushed open the door. She saw a little old lady sitting next to a funny machine with a big wheel going round and round.

"That looks fun!" said the princess.

"It *is* fun!" said the little old lady. "You push this bit with your foot and turn the big wheel and it makes lovely thread like this. Watch out though, because the needle is very . . ."

But it was too late. The princess had pricked her finger.

"Oh dear!" said the nice old lady. "I'll find a plaster."

"It's all right," said the princess. "It doesn't hurt. I just feel a little . . . sl . . . sl . . . sleepy."

Just then, The Seven Good Fairies came fluttering up the stairs.

"We're coming to find you!"

"Wherever has she gone?"

"Oh! Excuse me, madam. Have you seen— "

"Oh no . . . A SPINNING WHEEL!"

"We're too late. What can we do?"

"I know, let's wish EVERYONE asleep for a hundred years."

"Good idea, then we'll all wake up together!"

The seven fairies carried the princess and laid her carefully on her bed. Then they began to yawn. But, just before the fairies fell asleep, they made one last wish –

"Princess, princess, sleeping deep,
Only a prince can stir your sleep."

Before long, everyone in the palace had fallen under the sleeping spell – the servants, the cooks and the little dog in the kitchen. The Seven Good Fairies lay down all around the sleeping princess. When the jolly king and the thin queen returned from the festival, they began to feel sleepy too.

Outside, a magical forest of spiky thorns grew across the doors and around the palace walls until only the tallest towers could be seen. Every living thing in the palace slept.

They slept for ten years . . . they slept for twenty years . . . they slept for fifty years.

Sometimes, people would ask about the spiky thorn forest and the towers that rose above it. But everybody had forgotten about the jolly king and the thin queen and the sleeping beauty who lay inside.

They slept for eighty years . . . they slept for ninety years . . . they slept for a hundred years.

One day, a handsome young prince came riding by. He asked about the spiky thorn forest and the towers poking through it. An old man remembered something that his grandfather had told him about a beautiful princess, but it was all so long ago.

The prince liked the idea of the secret palace and the sleeping princess. He tied up his horse and began to cut his way through the thorns, but they were so thick and spiky that his sword became blunt. He was just about to turn away when a magical thing happened – every thorn changed into a lovely rose. The spiky forest opened into a path and the prince walked right up to the palace door.

The prince felt afraid, but he stepped slowly inside the hall, where cobwebs hung from every surface. The palace was completely silent except ... What was that noise? A gentle rumbling. He crept forward, and to his amazement, he saw snoozing servants, all gently snoring.

Then the prince found the jolly king and the thin queen, both sleeping deeply, and he realised that every one of the sleepers was dressed in clothes from a hundred years ago.

Again, the prince felt like turning and leaving that strange place, but something drew him to a bedroom.

The prince couldn't believe his eyes. He found seven tiny fairies fast asleep around a soft bed. And on the bed lay the most beautiful girl he had ever seen. Her clothes were also old-fashioned, but the prince couldn't help himself – he leant across and kissed her lightly on her forehead.

The spell was broken. The princess and the fairies woke and rubbed their eyes.

"That was a good sleep!"

"Except for your snoring."

"I wasn't snoring."

"Ooh! Who's this nice young man?"

"Looks like a prince to me."

"I think the princess and the prince should get married."

"Good idea! Let's have a wedding."

And so it was that the prince and princess got married. The jolly king and the thin queen were so happy, they had another party. They invited lots of kings and queens and The Seven Good Fairies and even the great-great-great-great-grandson of the frog.

This time they invited the bad fairy too. It had taken over a hundred years, but at last she had learnt how to be nice –

"May you be happy ever after.

My wish for you is love and laughter."

Hansel and Gretel and the Sticky Witch

H ansel and Gretel loved sweets. Sticky toffee chewy ones, crunchy munchy sugary ones, sweet fizzy sherbet ones and gooey melted chocolate ones. They just couldn't get enough.

Hansel and Gretel lived with their father, Hans, who loved his children very much. The truth is, they were rather spoilt.

"I'll be passing the shop on the way home," he would say. "Is there anything you'd like, my little sweeties?"

"Jelly beans," said Hansel, "fudge fingers, blackcurrant chews, chocolate monkey nuts and fizzy-wizzy colas."

"Happy hearts," said Gretel, "foam bananas, drumstick monster lollies, a cherry lipstick and grape-flavoured gobstoppers, please."

And every afternoon, Hansel and Gretel would rush out of the cottage to thank their kind father for the bags of sweeties, which always contained exactly what they had asked for.

Then they would sit outside the cottage, happily chewing and munching and licking until every last grain of sugar was gone.

But, one day, something peculiar happened. Their father called out as usual, "Hansel! Gretel! I'll be passing the

shop on the way home. Is there anything you'd like,
my little sweeties?"

And, as usual, Hansel and Gretel gave him a list of
all the yummy things they could think of –

"Sticky snacks."

"Lemon sherbets."

"Ice cream chews."

"Spaghetti gum."

At the end of the day, they ran to meet their father, their
tummies rumbling at the thought of all those lovely treats.
But, to their dismay, Hans had completely forgotten their
sweets. That night, poor Hansel and Gretel went to bed
without even a tiny jelly baby.

The same thing happened day after day, until one night the children said, "Father, every day you forget to buy our sweeties. Is something wrong?"

Their father smiled and stared dreamily at the moon.

"Oh no, my little sweeties," he giggled. "Everything is right! I have met a lovely lady, and I can't concentrate on anything else at all. Her name is Petal."

The children were very happy for their father and they suggested that Hans should bring Petal home to the cottage.

The next day, there was a gentle tap on the door and there stood Petal –

"Hello, Hans."

"Hello, Petal."

"Hello, Hansel."

"Hello, Gretel."

Petal was the nicest person the children had ever met. She had curly hair and when she smiled, her teeth were as white as pearls.

After she had gone, Hans was very keen to know what the children thought of his new girlfriend.

"Petal is lovely," said Hansel. "But why does she wear those white clothes?"

"Didn't you guess?" laughed Hans. "Petal is a dentist."

The days passed and at last Petal came to live in the little cottage. She cooked lovely healthy things to eat and, every morning and evening, she helped the children brush their teeth, top and bottom, front and back.

One night, Hansel could not sleep. He could hear Hans and Petal talking downstairs.

"Hans, I have something to tell you," said Petal.

"What is it, my pretty Petal?" asked Hans.

"It is Hansel and Gretel. Although they brush each night,

their teeth are not as white as they should be. It sounds cruel, but I think you should stop buying all those sweets."

Hans was very upset about not buying sweeties for his little children, but he knew that Petal was right, so at last he agreed.

In his little bed, Hansel was even more upset. He woke Gretel and told her what he had heard. The poor children could not imagine a life without rhubarb and custard chews. A small tear ran down Gretel's cheek.

"Don't cry, Gretel," said Hansel. "Look! I have a secret packet of humbugs hidden under my pillow. Tomorrow, we will go for a walk in the forest and eat them without anyone knowing."

Next morning, Hansel and Gretel told Hans and Petal they were going for a walk in the woods. Petal kissed them goodbye and made them promise to stick to the main path. When the cottage was out of sight, Hansel pulled out the enormous bag of humbugs and the two children wandered happily through the forest, sucking the lovely sugary sweets and crunching them between their teeth.

When they had eaten every last humbug, Hansel looked around and realised that they had wandered far from the main path and were completely lost.

"Don't worry, Hansel," said Gretel. "Look! I dropped my sweetie wrappers all through the forest. All we have to do is follow them and we will soon find our way home."

Hansel told his little sister that she should *never* drop litter, but he saw that as they picked up each sweet wrapper, they found their way home to the cottage, where Petal was waiting for them with a big smile and some new toothpaste.

The next day, Hans said, "I will be passing the shop on the way home, my little sweeties. Is there something you'd like? A nice pencil, perhaps?"

All morning, Hansel sat sadly in the garden, dreaming of bananaramas and pineapple chunks.

"Don't be sad, Hansel," said Gretel. "Look, I have a wonderful surprise which I was saving for your birthday . . . a huge bag of multicoloured glow-in-the-dark space whizzers. When Hans and Petal are asleep, we will creep outside and eat them in the forest."

So, that night, the naughty children slipped out of the window and set off into the woods. To make sure they would not get lost, clever Gretel left a trail of multicoloured glow-in-the-dark space whizzers all along the path.

At last, when they had eaten every last whizzer, the children turned to go home. They looked for the glowing trail that would lead them safely back, but to their dismay, the night animals had been following and had eaten every single one.

"Oh, Hansel," said Gretel, "the owls have waffled our whizzers. Now we will never find our way home. If only we had listened to Petal, we would be safely tucked up in our beds."

All night, the children wandered through the woods, cold and afraid. At last, they curled up under a tree and fell fast asleep.

Hansel had a funny dream. He imagined a delicious smell wafting through the forest. It smelt like gingerbread and honeycomb and melting chocolate. He opened his eyes and in front of him was the most amazing thing he had ever seen . . .

Behind a liquorice gate stood a candy cottage. The garden was filled with dolly mixture flowers. The roof, which was dripping with thick, thick chocolate, had whippy walnut chimney pots and chocolate raisins on the ridge. The walls were built of toffee bricks, stuck together with gooey jam, and the windows were shining barley sugar. The door was a huge bar of caramel and in the middle was an everlasting-gobstopper knocker.

Hansel and Gretel ran forward and began to break off pieces of the candy cottage and cram them into their mouths.

"Oh, Hansel!" cried Gretel. "The drainpipes are made of liquorice straws."

"Oh, Gretel!" cried Hansel. "The path is made of krazy kookie korners."

They ate and ate until their jaws
ached and their tummies were sore.
They were so busy chewing,
they didn't notice that a barley
sugar window had opened and
a strange old lady with pink
candyfloss hair had poked
her head outside –

"Who's that nibbling on my house,
     Greedy as a little mouse?
   Open up the caramel door.
 Come inside and eat some more."

Hansel and Gretel pulled open the door and crept slowly inside the candy cottage. They couldn't believe their eyes – from floor to ceiling were shelves stacked with boxes and jars overflowing with sweeties of every kind. Everything was carefully arranged in alphabetical order – acid drops, aniseed balls, apple bombs, bonbons, butterscotch . . . all the way through to whippy walnuts, yummy bars and zabba zoo gums. And, in the middle, stirring a big pot of gooey toffee, stood the little old lady dressed in candy colours, holding a stripy cane. She told them she was a famous candy maker who had made a fortune by selling sweets all over the world –

"Jelly beans and jiffy pops,
wonder worms and dippy drops.
I am called the Sticky Witch.
Making sweets has made me RICH!"

Then she laughed a horrible laugh and Hansel and Gretel could see right inside her sticky mouth! The Sticky Witch had crooked, gappy teeth as brown as toffee.

"Yuk!" shouted Hansel.

"Eek!" shouted Gretel.

They turned and ran out of the candy cottage, down the krazy kookie korners path, through the liquorice gate, into the forest and, by good luck, they found the path that led to their father's cottage.

"My dear little sweeties!" shouted Hans.

"Wherever have you been?" But Hansel and Gretel didn't answer. They were too busy scrubbing and brushing and polishing their teeth until they were as shiny and white as peppermint pearls.

"Lovely!" said Petal, patting their heads.

Deep in the woods, in the candy cottage, the Sticky Witch stirred her pot and made more and more delicious sweeties –

"Lemon lip-dippers, kitty kisses, pink pompoms, hunky herbets, gummy bums, kangaroo candy, piggy pops, charm bracelets, gooey eggs, sunny stripes, bonkers bars, strawberry starbites, curly cups, jawbreakers, smelly jelly bellyaches, goo-goo gums, bunny bubbles, swizzle fizzles, toffee toes . . ."